DOUBLE TROUBLE

by

May Garelick

Illustrated by Arthur Getz

Steve had his good days and bad days, just like all of us. Some days everything seemed to go wrong. Steve woke up with the sniffles one day and had to stay home from school. He was lonesome and his toys didn't look very interesting. Mother played with him for a while, but she was busy, too. Steve managed to get himself into trouble with both of his parents during those three days, each one worse than the last. Despite the aggravation, there was also humor and understanding when the confusion was resolved.

* *

Dewey Decimal Classification: Fic

About the Author:

MAY GARELICK has lived all over the United States, but she likes New York City, now her home, best of all. "I love the city," she says, "and the country can be pretty exciting, too. I like big adventure, but I think the biggest adventure of all is the one of day-to-day living, and so I wrote this story of an average boy and his life with his family in a city apartment." Miss Garelick is an editor for a publishing house, and the co-author of two cookbooks for children.

About the Illustrator:

ARTHUR GETZ also lives in New York City but he was born in the neighboring state of New Jersey. After school he got a job summers as a seaman aboard a freighter between New York and West Africa. The money he earned on these trips paid for his art studies at Pratt Institute in Brooklyn. He was a Lieutenant in the Army in World War II, serving in the Philippines. He has painted murals and does many covers for *The New Yorker* magazine. His verse has also appeared in that magazine. He is married and has two children.

double trouble

by May Garelick

ILLUSTRATED BY ARTHUR GETZ

1963 FIRST CADMUS EDITION
THIS SPECIAL EDITION IS PUBLISHED BY ARRANGEMENT WITH
THE PUBLISHERS OF THE REGULAR EDITION
THOMAS Y. CROWELL COMPANY
BY
E. M. HALE AND COMPANY
EAU CLAIRE, WISCONSIN

For Paul Scott
who once let me in on a secret

and for Peter Zelin
who will know why

WEDNESDAY

off to a bad start...

CHAPTER 1

Rain. Rain. Would it ever stop?

"With those sniffles, Stevie," his mother had said at breakfast, "you'd better stay home from school today."

"Yippee," Steve had cheered.

But now, after a few hours, he was fed up. It was boring at home with everyone away, especially his best friend, Jerry.

Steve and Jerry lived in the same apartment house. They went to the same school, rode together on the school bus, and were in the same class. After school they played together until Jerry's mother came home from work.

Even though they were best friends—

almost always together, almost as if they were brothers—they liked to do different things.

Jerry liked to make things. He could stay in the house for hours making clay

people or horses. He cut things out of paper, and he made animals out of soap.

Steve liked to make things, too. But he'd get impatient. "Let's go out and have a catch," Steve would soon say to Jerry. And they'd run down to the playground. After all, Jerry liked to play ball as much as anybody.

Steve looked up at the clock in his room. It would be hours before Jerry came home from school. What could he do by himself?

True, his mother was home. But she was always busy doing one thing or another. When Steve wandered into the kitchen, she was ironing.

6

"No, Stevie. You can't play ball in the outside hall," she said. "It's too drafty."

So Steve wandered back to his room. What is there to do if you can't go out? What can you do all alone?

I know, he decided, looking at his cars. I'll make a traffic jam.

CHAPTER 2

Even though Steve was eight years old, he still liked to play with his cars.

Steve had many cars—cars enough to make the biggest traffic jam you ever saw. He had a red convertible, a yellow taxi-cab, a black-and-white police car, a

double-decker bus, and some regular buses. Besides these, he had a fire engine, an ambulance, a dig-and-dump truck, and a good-sized tow truck. With his cars, Steve could tie up traffic from his house on 22nd Street all the way to 222nd Street.

Most of his cars he had had since he was little. Some were new.

Every once in a while, when his mother was straightening his room, she'd say: "Stevie, why don't you give a few of

your old cars to your cousin Timmy? You've had them since you were four!"

"No, Ma. I need them!" And he did. He needed them for traffic jams.

That's it. That's what he would do. Make a traffic jam.

C R A S H

Toot-a-toot

CRASH

E R R R U U M N M N

Beep, beep

Toot-a-toot

T O O O O O O O T

Cars piled up on cars, jamming into each other. Traffic was at a standstill.

Steve put on his policeman's cap and white gloves. Ready!

With the help of the tow truck he moved the disabled car off the highway. Then he lined up the cars and set them on their way. That was that. Traffic was moving freely again.

What next?

He took off his policeman's outfit and put on his flier's cap and goggles.

"Pilot to navigator," he called.

"Navigator to pilot," he answered.

"Did you say something, Stevie?" called his mother from the kitchen.

"Pilot to navigator," he replied.

"Oh—?" said his mother.

"We're off," called Steve.

But his airplane didn't take off.

Steve remembered that the other night, when he was playing navigator-to-pilot with his father, the plane hadn't worked.

well. His father had promised to fix it when he had more time.

Now Steve tried. He tried again and again, but he couldn't make it fly.

"Shoot," he muttered in anger, and threw the plane on the bed in disgust.

Just then there was a tremendous clap of thunder. Steve wasn't particularly afraid of thunder. But this was such a long, loud roll that it frightened him. He hunched up his shoulders, picked up his plane, and dashed into the kitchen.

"Ma, what time is Dad coming home?"

"Late," she answered. "He's working late tonight."

"My plane won't fly," complained Steve. "Can you fix it, Ma?"

14

"I don't know a thing about planes, Stevie," said his mother. She was still ironing. The basket near her ironing board was piled high with laundry. It looked as if she would never be finished.

The kitchen was cozy and warm. There was soft music coming from the radio and sweet smells of a pie baking in the oven.

Steve got up on the stepladder chair and looked out.

The rain was coming down in buckets, lashing against the window. In front of the house the one tree swayed back and forth in the strong wind. The tree's branches, heavy with rain, bent low.

15

They brushed against the little fence around the tree trunk.

"That round fence looks like the basket in the Hidden Treasure game. The basket at Jane's house where I found the magic set," said Steve. "You know, Ma, even if Jane didn't get such wonderful presents, it was a pretty good birthday."

"Why, she got some lovely things," said his mother in a surprised tone.

"No," said Steve. "Mostly clothes. The flippers and the dart game. . . . They were the only good presents. Mom, can I have a dart game like Jane's?" he asked as an afterthought.

"Oh Stevie. With the cars and the toys, the games and the hats—where could

you put another thing in that room of yours?" she asked patiently.

"On the wall, Ma. A dart game hangs on the wall. It doesn't take up any room," Steve answered seriously.

His mother smiled.

"We'll see," she said as she reached into the oven and took out a steaming apple pie.

"Yummy! Can I have a piece of pie?" asked Steve.

"After dinner. We'll have dessert with

Dad. How about a glass of orange juice instead?"

"I'm not thirsty," pouted Steve.

"Why don't you practice your magic tricks," suggested his mother.

"It's no fun by yourself," he sulked.

"Tell you what," said his mother. "I'll just iron this one shirt. Then you can try your magic on me."

"If I had a dart game," said Steve, "you wouldn't have to stop ironing. I could play darts by myself."

"That's all right. I don't mind," she answered. "As a matter of fact, I like magic tricks."

"Wish we could play the Hidden Treasure game right now," said Steve.

20

Everyone at Jane's party had played the Hidden Treasure game. The grownups, too. It was a good game, but it wasn't easy to find the hidden treasure.

First a grownup has to hide something. Then the children have to hunt for it. You know what the hidden thing is, but you have no clues for finding it.

When you come near the hidden thing, the grownups clap their hands and call *hot, hot, hot.* If you are not near it, they say *cold, cold,* low and slow. Whoever finds the treasure, it's his to keep. That's how you play the Hidden Treasure game.

The magic set had been the hidden treasure. Steve was the one who had found it, hidden under a newspaper in the wastebasket at Jane's house.

"What are you dreaming about, Stevie?" asked his mother. "Bring on the magic."

"I was just thinking how hard it was to find the magic set," said Steve. He jumped off his perch on the stepladder chair and started back to his room.

The apartment Steve lived in was not very big, but it was spread out. First there was a small alcove. That's where you left your rubbers when it was raining, and your umbrella in the umbrella stand. Then there was the kitchen and the

22

living room. When you came out of the living room, you came to a hallway. Then his parents' room, and way at the end was Steve's room.

A person could do a lot of thinking on the way from the kitchen to Steve's room. Anybody could get sidetracked. Especially Steve. His mind was on the Hidden Treasure game. Nothing else mattered.

CHAPTER 3

Suppose I hide something and let the *grownups* look for it, Steve said to himself as he sauntered down the hall. Something valuable, worth looking for. They'd play tonight. Just to find it.

In his parents' room there were valuable things, many valuable things.

When he was little, his parents used to say: "Don't touch this," or "You'll drop that. Be careful." Well, now he didn't drop things. He was careful.

There, on the dresser, was his mother's gold watch. Her mother—that is to say, Steve's grandmother—had given it to her as a sixteenth-birthday present. She'd had it ever since. She took very good care of it and never wore it when she worked around the house. But, if she started out the door without it, she'd say: "Oops, I can't go out without my watch. I'd feel undressed."

Sometimes, if his mother couldn't remember where she'd left her watch, his father would help her look until they found it.

The watch, decided Steve. That was the valuable thing he would hide.

Handling it carefully so as not to drop

it, Steve looked around for a good safe place to hide the watch. Safe, but hard to find.

"Easy does it," he said. And he gently slipped the watch into the small picnic basket in the hall closet.

"I'll get it, Ma," yelled Steve when he heard the doorbell.

"Saved by the bell," said his mother. "If that's Jerry, I'll keep on with my ironing," she added as Steve ran past her to open the door.

"Hi," said Jerry, and he let fly a piece of paper.

When the plane landed, Jerry picked it up. "Made it in school today," he said as he held it high over his head and let it fly again. "Zoom."

Steve looked on enviously. "Wish I'd been in school today."

"Shucks, I can show you how to make one. It's easy. See? All you need is a long piece of paper," he said, opening out the

28

plane. "See?" he repeated. "You fold it like this, and this, and this, and it's a plane. Here, you fly it," he added.

"I'll go get some paper and make one too," said Steve. Just at that moment the downstairs bell rang.

"Oops, three short rings. That's my grandma," called Jerry to Steve. "Have to go now. I'm getting new sneakers. Maybe I'll see you later. 'By, Mrs. Green," he waved and tore out the door.

Poor Stevie, thought his mother. If he complains now about having no one to play with, I couldn't blame him a bit, she said to herself as she folded up the ironing board.

But Steve didn't complain. Instead he came scooting happily into the kitchen.

"I know how to make a plane," he said. "A plane that will fly. It's paper, but it'll fly."

"Fine," said his mother as she picked up a pile of ironed shirts.

"I'm going to make one now, Ma."

"There's a pad of paper," she said, pointing with her chin to a pad under the cupboard.

"No, that's no good. Jerry said it has to be a long piece of paper," said Steve, and he ran down the hall.

CHAPTER 4

Steve looked around on his father's desk. He found a piece of paper that seemed to be just right. He folded it down the middle, folded back the sides, and "Zoom," he said. But it didn't fly.

"Not enough breeze in here," he grumbled as he opened the window.

The rain had stopped. A strong gust of wind swept into the room. "Let 'er go," said Steve. But even with the breeze in the room, the plane took a nose dive and dropped to the floor.

"Out the window," he said aloud, his anger mounting. "That wind out there would make even this crummy plane fly." And, with all his strength, he let it sail.

But even outside, in the strong wind, the plane fell, plop. It landed on the hedge in front of the house. Steve rushed into the kitchen, complaining to his mother.

"But I don't know how to make a paper plane," she said. "Well—let's see. Maybe I can." She took a sheet of paper from the pad and tried.

She wasn't fooling. She didn't know how to make a plane.

"Oh, Ma!" said Steve irritably. "Jerry said it has to be a *long* piece of paper."

34

"Maybe it tells how to make a paper plane in your book on folding paper," she said. "Get the book, Stevie."

When he came back with the book, Steve muttered hopelessly, "I wish Dad were home."
His mother ran her finger down the page of *Things to Make.* "My, there's a whole chapter on airplanes."

"Wow, some of them look hard! Let's make the glider, Mom. It looks something like Jerry's. Doesn't the paper have to be long?" asked Steve.

"Long*ish*," she said. "I'll read the directions and we'll each make a plane. It'll work out, you'll see."

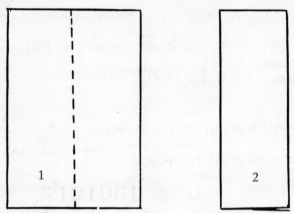

1. Fold paper down middle, the long way.
2. Folded paper will look like this.

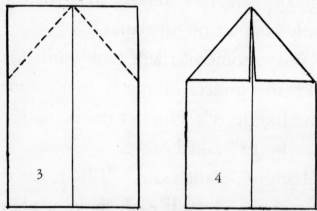

3. Open out. Fold corners, following dotted lines.
4. Paper will look like this.

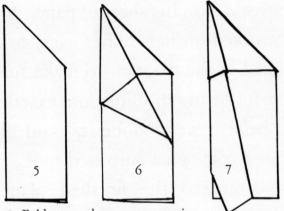

5. Fold paper down center again.
6. Fold one side out from tip to line up with center fold.
7. Fold same side out again.

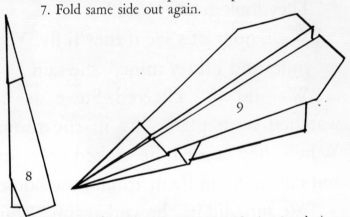

8. Turn paper over. Make same two folds (as 6 and 7) on other side. Be sure folds are well creased.
9. Plane will look like this. Zoom!

Steve worked on his sheet of paper; his mother worked on hers. After every fold they looked at the diagram to make sure they were following the directions exactly.

"I do believe we've done it," said his mother in a somewhat surprised tone.

Steve compared the finished planes with the picture.

"They look great, Mom!"

"Well, now let's see if they'll fly. You try yours and I'll try mine," she said.

"We did it," cheered Steve as he watched both planes fly in the room. When they landed, he picked them up and ran zooming them around the house.

"We sure did it!" he said again. "Wait 'til Jerry sees *these*. Zoom," he called, flying first one plane and then the other down the hallway.

"Coming in for a landing," boomed Steve.

"Roger and over," answered his mother. Steve smiled at her and winked.

CHAPTER 5

Steve's mother was glad to see him smiling and happy again. She was pleased, too, that she had been able to help him make the paper planes.

"As a matter of fact, the instructions weren't hard to follow," she said half aloud.

"What?" asked Steve.

"Nothing. Guess we'd better have our dinner," she answered.

"What about Dad?"

"He's having a dinner meeting after work."

"I'm starved, Mom."

"I know. I'll hurry it up," she said.

His mother knew that, when Steve was hungry, nothing interested him as much as eating, not even planes.

"It's a good thing you stayed home from school today," she said as she put a baked potato on Steve's plate. "You nipped the sniffles, didn't get a cold, and you'll be in fine shape for school tomorrow."

"What's for dessert, Ma?"

"The pie. But let's wait for Dad and have our dessert together," she suggested.

"Let's just have a small piece now, and

42

the rest later," was Steve's suggestion.

His mother smiled as she put a thin piece of pie on a small plate.

"Wish Dad would hurry home," said Steve.

"Won't be long now," said his mother, clearing the table.

"The pie is great, Ma," said Steve, his face brightening as he heard the familiar scratching sound at the door. He knew that welcome sound. It was his father letting himself in.

CHAPTER 6

His father burst into the house as if he had been running nonstop all the way from his office. "Get your coat, Steve," he said breathlessly. "There's a five-alarm fire in a factory building down the street."

"No, Joe, not tonight," Steve's mother said to her husband. "He was home from school today and . . ."

"Oh, Ma, please let me go," pleaded Steve. "You said I was better."

"We won't be long," promised his

45

father as he kissed his wife on the cheek.

"Please, Ma?" Steve begged.

"Well," she said slowly, "put your sweater on. And your muffler too. And, if you feel cold, come right back."

"Sure, Ma, we will," promised Steve, running to his room for his sweater.

"Hurry," called his father. "Why don't you come with us, Mary? Do you good to get out."

"Thank you, no. I don't like to watch a building burn," said Steve's mother.

"We're not going to *watch it burn*, either! We're going to watch the firemen *keep* it from burning," he answered.

"I never thought of it that way," she said. "Still, I think I'll stay home."

There were many things the family liked to do together. But going to fires was not one of them. "Strictly for the men in the family," said his father, nudging Steve.

"Remember, you two. The firemen can manage without you," Steve's mother called after them. "You don't have to wait until they put the fire out."

"We won't. We'll stay just long enough to make sure they get the fire under control," he laughed. "Back in half an hour," he added.

Steve and his father ran down the street in the direction of the fire. The street was crowded. It looked as if everyone in the neighborhood were either on his way to the fire, or there already. At some distance from the burning building people stood behind police barriers watching.

Firemen were pulling hoses down the street. Other firemen were running with axes. Up against the factory building were several ladders. Firemen were on the ladders, dousing the flames. Smoke was billowing out of the building.

"Look at those firemen work," said Steve's father.

"They're the best," said a man who was standing next to his father. "They've been at it for hours."

"Were there any people in the building?" Steve's father asked.

"No. And it's a good thing, too,"

answered the man. "That building looks like a firetrap to me."

"See that truck, Steve?" his father asked. "A Salvation Army truck. Hot coffee and sandwiches for the firemen."

"And what's that?" asked Steve, pointing to a tank on the sidewalk.

"An oxygen tank. If a fireman is overcome by smoke, they revive him with oxygen from the tank."

Next to the oxygen tank was a cot, and a truck with more cots inside.

"They don't always have these things for every fire," said Steve.

"No," said his father. "Nor do they often have fires as big as this.

"It'll be some time before they get that

fire under control. But our time's up. Let's start back."

Steve looked around, trying to think up some more questions. He knew that his father wanted him to know things. His father liked to answer questions. Secretly, Steve knew this was one way he could get his father to stay out longer.

"Come on," said his father, who was on to Steve's tricks. "There's plenty going on around here. All very interesting, but we did promise."

"Five more minutes, Dad?" pleaded Steve.

"No sir!" said his father emphatically. "You know I don't go for that five-more-minute routine. Five leads to ten, and ten to an argument. So let's go, right now. Race you back to the house."

That was the nice thing about his

father. If he made Steve stop doing something, he thought of another interesting thing to take its place.

They raced back.

"You let me win, Pop. I know it," complained Steve. That was all right to do when he was little, but now he didn't like it if his father let him win.

"Oh no, I didn't. I'm pooped, that's all," said his father, puffing.

"There's pie for dessert," announced Steve as he pushed the elevator button.

"See—we weren't long," said his father when they came into the apartment.

"Medals for both of you—on your plates," said Steve's mother.

They weren't medals. They were two

big pieces of pie. And, as an extra surprise, there was ice cream on the pie. For
herself, Steve's mother took a small piece

of pie with just a dab of ice cream. "My diet," she explained.

"How was your meeting?" she asked her husband.

"Fine. Just fine," answered Steve's father. "The new man will be a great help to us all."

"What's his name, Dad?" asked Steve.

"Mr. Singer, Paul Singer," he replied.

Steve knew the people who worked in his father's office, and he knew about their work. He had been to his father's office many times. And he knew about the new man who was coming to work with his father.

"How about getting ready for bed," said his father.

"For bed?" asked Steve. "It's early, Dad."

"Not so early," said his mother.

"Can I just show Dad how to make a plane?" Steve stalled.

"Go along, Steve. Get ready for bed. I'll be right with you. You'll show me later."

CHAPTER 7

Generally, when Steve was in bed, his father came to his room. They would either read a story together or talk for a while until Steve became sleepy.

Tonight, he'd show his father how to make a paper plane.

"Ready, Dad!" he called eagerly, as soon as he'd climbed into bed.

"Mary," his father called, "did you mail the rent check?"

"No," answered Steve's mother.

"That's odd. I left it right here on the desk this morning," said his father.

Steve got out of bed and went to his parents' room. He stood in the doorway, watching his father riffle through the papers on his desk.

"I left it right here," his father repeated. "I know I did. Steve," he asked sternly, "did you see a check on my desk?"

Steve wasn't exactly sure. His father's sharp tone frightened him. "No," he said softly.

"That doesn't sound very convincing," said his father. "Are you *sure* you didn't see the check?"

"Oh, Joe," said Steve's mother, coming

60

into the room. "He probably doesn't even know what a check is."

"He knows all right. Steve, did you see a piece of paper that looks like this?" asked his father, showing him a check.

"What would he *do* with a check, anyway?" asked Steve's mother.

It came to Steve in a flash. That old airplane he'd sent flying out the window! That paper plane that couldn't even fly. *That* was his father's check. "It landed on the hedge," said Steve, almost in a whisper. "Maybe it's still there."

"It landed on the hedge? What are you talking about?" asked his father.

"The paper plane," explained Steve. "The one that didn't fly."

61

His father gave Steve a piercing look as he opened the window.

"Jerry said it had to be a long piece of paper. I didn't notice it had any writing on it," said Steve, joining his father.

Steve's mother came over to the window. They all looked out. There was nothing on the hedge. No sign of the plane.

"I'll go down and look for it," volunteered Steve, eager for a chance to get out of this situation.

"Can't you call the bank in the morning and stop the check?" Steve's mother asked her husband.

"That's not the point," he answered. "He has every conceivable kind of toy.

63

Why does he have to make planes out of checks?"

"My real plane wouldn't fly," protested Steve.

"I told you I'd fix it when I had the time. Why are you so impatient? Why does everything have to be done right then and there, the very minute you want it?"

"Joe, dear," said Steve's mother. "We can't blame him for something he doesn't know." She was still sure Steve didn't know about checks. "We should have explained to him that a check is as important as money," she continued. "He can't know if we don't explain."

"Explain! Explain! How can you know

what's coming up next?" exploded his father. He was terribly angry.

Steve felt awful. "I'm sorry, Dad," he said quietly. He went back to his room, closed his door, and got into bed.

There was a knock at his door.

"Come in," said Steve in a low voice.

When his father came in, Steve was crying. "Dad, I didn't mean to throw out the check," he said.

"I know you didn't," said his father. "And I'm sorry I lost my temper."

"You said you'd fix my plane, Dad. You promised. I'm not impatient."

"Everyone is impatient, once in a while. Grownups, too," said his father. "And sometimes we're impatient with our children. When we expect them to know what grownups know. . . ."

"I *know* that a check is as important as money," interrupted Steve. "I just didn't notice it was a check."

"*You* should have been more careful and noticed," said his father gently. "And *I* should have been more careful and put the check in the drawer." He sat down on the edge of Steve's bed. "In a way, we're both at fault—you and I. Sleepy?" he asked.

"Yes," murmured Steve as he sat up to kiss his father goodnight.

"Mary," called his father.

Steve's mother came into the room.

"I'll call the bank in the morning and

stop the check," she said, turning to her husband. Then she leaned down and whispered in Steve's ear: "Feel better now?"

Steve nodded.

She kissed his ear and turned out the light.

THURSDAY

double trouble...

CHAPTER 8

When Steve opened his eyes the next morning, the first thing he thought about was the check. But it didn't bother him.

He climbed out of bed. There, on the table, was his airplane. He let it fly. Perfect. His father had fixed it last night.

"Stevie, are you awake?" asked his mother when she came into his room.

Steve grinned.

"And how is everything this brisk, sunny day?" she said, pulling up the window shades. "By the way, Steve," she added, "have you seen my watch any-where around?"

"Yep," he answered and let his plane fly again.

"Good. I was afraid I'd lost it," she said happily. "Where'd you see it?"

Steve remembered he had hidden the watch. But he couldn't remember exactly where. He said nothing. He was thinking.

"Where is it?" asked his mother again. "I've searched and searched for it."

"I hid it," said Steve.

"You hid it?" she asked. "Why?"

"For the game," he answered. "I wanted you and Dad to play the Hidden Treasure game. To see if you could find the watch."

"Oh you did, eh?" his mother said

72

playfully. "Well, sir, we've no time for games this morning. Please hand over the watch, young man."

"I can't remember exactly where I hid it," Steve answered quietly.

"Come on, Stevie. Think hard. Try to remember," she urged.

He was thinking, but he could not remember.

"Maybe Jerry knows," Steve brightened. "I'll go ask him. No—Jerry came in after—on account of him—I can't remember now. But don't worry, Ma. It's safe."

"Stevie, I don't know what's come over you lately! Throwing out checks, hiding watches." His mother's voice became a bit sharp. "You come right home from school," she added, "and search until you find it."

"But Ma, Jerry and I are supposed to go over to Bill's today. You said I could."

"How is it you can remember that? Jerry can go without you," she said.

"But you promised, Ma."

His mother was stern now.

"And this is one time I'm going to break my promise. We've been much too easygoing with you lately," she said as she walked out of Steve's room.

Easy? thought Steve. Life couldn't be harder. First one trouble. Now another.

He finished dressing.

Breakfast that morning was a solemn

affair. His mother talked to his father. His father talked to her. Neither one paid any attention to Steve.

"Ma? I promised Bill. It's not his fault that I can't remember where I hid the watch," tried Steve again.

His mother went right on clearing the dishes off the kitchen table. She didn't say another word.

Steve gave up. It was no use. The less said, the better.

" 'By," he said when he left for school.

"Good-by," she answered.

CHAPTER 9

On the bus Steve told Jerry about the check and about the missing watch. "That crummy old plane," he said. "Made me forget where I hid the watch."

"Heck, you'll find it. Where'd you look?" asked Jerry.

"I haven't looked. I have to go straight home from school. Just to look. That's why my mother won't let me go to Bill's."

During school Steve forgot about the

watch. It never crossed his mind again until he and Jerry were standing in front of the bus after school.

"I'll tell Bill why you can't come," said Jerry. "So long," he added. "Hope you find the watch."

"Big help!" said Steve.

On the way home he didn't talk to any of the children on the bus. When he got home, he didn't stop to see who was in the playground. He went right upstairs.

"Hi, Mom."

"Hi," she answered. She was still upset.

Not everyone could tell when his mother was upset. But Steve could. He always knew. She didn't yell. She didn't pick on him. She just stopped talking.

Anything she had to say, she said in few words, and in a strict tone.

Better start the search, thought Steve.

He didn't know where to begin. He looked around the living room. He wandered aimlessly back to his room. He looked out the window. The boys were playing ball. Steve stood at the window for a few seconds.

Where could that watch be? He sauntered back to the living room.

"Ma, how does a person get to remember something?" he asked.

"I don't know," she answered.

"If you forget a thing, how does it sometimes pop back into your head?"

"You keep thinking about it. What were you doing before you hid it? What happened later? Try to think. It'll come to you. If you want to remember, you will," she said gently.

"Oh Ma, I do want to remember— honest!"

His mother said nothing. But maybe she was right. It bothered him to think about the watch. In a way, he wanted to

80

forget it. When he thought about it, it made him sad. Maybe it would pop back into his head when he least expected it. This sometimes happened.

Steve walked back to his room.

His eye caught the poem that was pinned on the door. Although he knew it by heart, Steve stood there reading:

A DOOR? WHAT FOR?

If you didn't have a door
That closed off your room
From the ceiling to the floor
You could hear what we said
After we'd sent you to bed.
Why do you want a door?
What in the world is it for?

When Steve was little he didn't like it if they closed his door. He felt he was missing something. But lately, even if he was just playing in his room, he would close his door. A few weeks ago, when Steve was sick, his father had said: "We'll leave the door open tonight, so we can hear you if you call." But Steve had insisted that he wanted the door closed. That was when his father had made up the poem.

"Write it down, Pa?" Steve had asked him.

His father did.

Later Steve answered by writing in the margin, and then he pinned the poem up on the door:

I need a door
to hide behind
if I want to.
That's what a door is for.
To hide behind.

"Hide? Yipe!" called Steve. And he looked hopefully behind the door.

"Did you find it?" called his mother, just as hopefully.

"Nope," he said softly as he came into the living room and looked out the window. The boys were still playing ball.

"Ma? Okay if I go down for a while?" asked Steve.

"No," she answered definitely.

He knew better than to ask. But no harm in trying.

Thursday afternoon. There probably wouldn't even be anything good on television, he thought. Anyway she wouldn't let him look at TV. He was being punished.

Sometimes, when she punished him, his mother forgot about the punishment. But today, she just sat there reading her book. She didn't even look up at him.

Steve kicked the leg of the sofa.

"Now just a minute, young man. Let's get one thing straight," said his mother. "You are staying in to find the watch that *you* hid. Please don't act as if you are being picked on."

"But why do you have to stop talking to me?" asked Steve sulkily. "I didn't break the watch. I just can't remember where I put it. Is that so terrible?"

"It is terrible," answered his mother. "And don't sulk. We've told you and told you not to fool around with valuable things. Checks and watches are not play-things. I tell you right now, Steve. If that watch is lost—"

"Ma—" interrupted Steve, "it's not lost."

"All right, then find it. That's all I ask of you."

Steve stalked out of the living room.

CHAPTER 10

The family was no sooner seated at the dinner table that evening than his father asked: "What made you decide that the watch was the thing to hide?"

"It had to be a valuable thing, so you'd play the game," explained Steve.

"Let's see. Could you have hidden it in the living room? In a box? In a bowl? Try to remember," his father coaxed. "How will you know if we're hot or cold if you don't know the hiding place?" he asked playfully.

His father was out to help him. Steve could see that. Still, he couldn't remember a single clue.

"Oh well, if you say you hid it in the house, it's still in the house. It'll turn up. Wait a minute," his father sang out. "Reconstruct the crime. We'll play the game right now! Steve, you hide my cigarette case. Mother and I will hunt for it."

While Steve looked for a place to hide the cigarette case, he heard his father say: "Perhaps he'll hide it where he hid the watch."

"I sure hope so," said Steve, perking up.

Steve thought a long time. He picked a hiding place. Then he looked around to see if the watch was there. He picked another hiding place and looked around some more. No watch.

Maybe they'll find the watch while they search for the case, thought Steve.

"Ready!" he called enthusiastically.

His mother looked. His father looked.

"Cold, cold," whispered Steve.

There was giggling and laughing, hunting and searching. Steve stood in front of the hiding place. His mother got behind him.

"Hot, hot, hot," yelled Steve.

She found the case. But no watch.

"Too bad," said his father. "It'll turn up. Let's forget about it for now."

All evening they tried to act as if it didn't matter that the watch was missing.

But Steve knew it mattered. He knew they were still upset, especially his mother.

90

FRIDAY

in-and-out of trouble...

CHAPTER 11

Steve's mother came to school early Friday morning. She had never come to school before, except during open-school week. She talked to his teacher. His teacher nodded and beckoned to Steve.

As soon as Steve and his mother were out of the classroom, his mother asked, "What have you done with my eyeglasses?"

Her eyeglasses? He hadn't seen her eyeglasses.

93

I'm in for it now, thought Steve. Now everytime anything is missing they'll blame me. But aloud, all he said was, "I didn't touch your glasses, Ma."

Steve had a bad day at school. When he came home with Jerry, his mother said, "Hi, Jerry." Not a word to Steve.

"Really, Ma," said Steve, "I hid your watch, but I didn't hide your glasses."

"Steve," she said, "forgetting is one thing. Lying is another. I hope you're not lying."

"I'm not lying," said Steve.

"Good," she said. But it seemed to Steve that she didn't believe him.

"I'm going in to take a shower. You

boys play in Steve's room. I don't want you messing up the living room," she said.

"We'd better not," said Steve to Jerry when his mother was out of the room. "Not today! Honest, Jerry. I didn't even see her glasses. I sure wish I could find that watch. Because if I don't, I'll get blamed for everything."

"Come on," said Jerry. "I'll help you. I'm a good finder. I find lots of things. "

Jerry got up on a chair in front of Steve's closet. He threw the hats from the shelf onto the bed.

"No watch up here," he said. "Heave them back."

"Later," said Steve as he crawled under the dresser. "Let's keep on looking.

Jerry," he asked, peeking out, "what was the worst, the most terrible thing you ever did in your whole life?"

"One time—" said Jerry slowly, "once I smoked one of my grandfather's cigars."

"You didn't!" gasped Steve as he crawled out from under the dresser.

"Yup, I did," answered Jerry.

"Didn't it make you choke?"

"Not too much," answered Jerry.

"Did you ever smoke again?"

"Nah. Don't care for it much."

"What did your mother do when she found out?" asked Steve.

"She didn't find out. And she won't if you don't tell her. And you'd better not," warned Jerry.

Steve didn't like being threatened. "I never tell a secret!" he said.

"And don't you go telling *your* mother, either," said Jerry.

Now Steve was getting angry. "What if I do tell her? I don't keep secrets from *my* mother," said Steve.

"But it's not your secret, and you'd better promise that you won't tell it," threatened Jerry.

"Okay," sulked Steve. "Come on, let's try and find that watch. On account of you and that old paper plane I got into two troubles. First the check—"

"Just a sec'," Jerry cut in. "Don't blame me, bud, or I'll stop looking."

Now they were pulling things out of the dresser. Every drawer was opened. The bed was piled high with shirts, underwear, and socks.

"Jerry," asked Steve, "how come you're afraid to tell your mother that you smoke?"

"I'm not afraid. I just don't want to," answered Jerry. "And I don't smoke. I told you I don't like it."

Steve was silent. "I think my mother hates me," he said after a while.

"You're bugs," said Jerry. "Mothers don't hate their children."

"Oh no? Then why should she think I'm lying when I'm telling her the honest truth?" asked Steve.

"That's the way they are," said Jerry. "You do one thing wrong—and wham! Everything is your fault. They get over it, though."

"Not my mother. When she gets mad, she stays mad," said Steve. "Why should she stop talking to me, just because—"

"Stevie, Stevie darling," called his mother from the bathroom.

"Uh oh. Now I'm gonna catch it for

the mess," said Steve to Jerry. He grabbed up an armful of clothes and was stuffing them into the drawer.

"Stevie darling," his mother said as she threw her arms around him. She hugged him and kissed him.

"Oh, Ma," said Steve, embarrassed. Jerry looked on in amazement.

"I found my glasses," she said. "They were right here in my bathrobe pocket. Please, please forgive me. I'm terribly sorry." And again she hugged him. "Whatever got into me?" she continued. "I feel horrible for blaming you." And once again she kissed Steve.

"All right, Ma."

All this hugging and kissing in front of

Jerry. "I'm glad you found your glasses," said Steve solemnly. "Wish we could find the watch too."

She laughed, "Well, that makes it even Steven. One for one. You forgot where you'd put the watch. I forgot where I'd put my glasses. Everyone forgets things. Not only children. We'll find the watch, too. I'm sure we will."

As she talked, she carefully put the clothes back into the dresser drawers. "Hand me the rest of the things," she said. "Then you boys run down to the playground."

"So long, Mom," waved Steve happily. "I'll come up with Dad."

"Very good." His mother smiled.

"You see?" said Jerry to Steve when they were out the door. "They get over—"

"Jerry," Steve interrupted. "See? That's why I think you should tell your mother about the smoking. They get mad, but they get over it."

That evening the family had a fine dinner: lamb chops, baked potatoes, and peas. For dessert, ice cream and fresh strawberries. Steve's favorites.

His mother brought the coffee and hot chocolate into the living room, just as if they were having company.

Everyone was in a relaxed, easy mood.

His father was reading his newspaper. Steve was on the floor working in his puzzle book. Steve's mother turned on the radio.

"What a week!" she said. "I'm glad it's behind us. And today was the worst day of all."

"Today started out terrible, but it turned out to be a good day," said Steve.

"That's how days go," said his father. "Sometimes good, sometimes bad. Most are good, though. The thing to do is to get over the bad days and enjoy the good ones."

"Where are we going tomorrow?" asked Steve.

"Got any ideas?" asked his father.

"Not really," said Steve.

"Let's wait and see how the weather

turns out. We can decide tomorrow," said his father.

"In the meantime," said Steve's mother, "it's time to get ready for a good night's sleep; to bed with you."

SATURDAY

all's well that ends well...

CHAPTER 12

Steve and his father spent Saturdays together. In the morning there were family chores to be done. Steve's mother had her jobs. Steve and his father had theirs. They picked up the laundry, or the shoes at the shoemaker's. They returned books to the library. Or, if his father had special work to do at the office, Steve went with him.

When the morning chores were done, Steve and his father would go off together for the afternoon.

109

"How does it look, Dad?" asked Steve proudly, very pleased with the job he had done on the inside of the car.

"Excellent! And what do you think of this?" asked his father, waving his hand over the outside.

"Ditto!" said Steve. "We'll have the cleanest car in the neighborhood. Where are we going this afternoon?" he asked.

"On this particular Saturday we'll let Mom come with us. As a matter of fact, it's her surprise."

"Just about done," said Steve's mother as they came into the house. "Joe," she said to her husband, "will you get the picnic basket, please?"

110

"A picnic?" said Steve. "Goody—I'll go get the basket, Mom."

"In the hall closet," she called.

Steve took down the basket. Something in it was rattling around. He opened it. Well, no wonder. Inside were a thermos jug, a few plastic plates, cups, and some spoons.

Steve carried the basket to the kitchen.

He watched his mother as she took everything out and lined the bottom of the basket with a dish towel. She poured grape juice into the thermos. Then she put the wrapped food into the basket. "Golden brown chicken," she said.

"Mmnn," said Steve, smacking his lips.

"This basket is much too big," said his mother. "The smaller one would pack better."

"I'll get it, Mom."

Steve ran to the hall closet.

"Yipe," he yelled suddenly. "Ma, Ma, Mom!" he called. "Guess what, Ma!" he shouted, bolting toward the kitchen as if he'd been stung by a bee. "Guess what!"

"What's the matter? What's hap-

pened?" she asked as she ran toward him. "What's the trouble?"

"No trouble, Mom. I found it."

His father was standing in the hallway, his face covered with shaving soap. "Found it?" he asked. "Was the basket lost too?"

"No, Dad. The watch!" explained Steve. "I found it. In this picnic basket. That's where I hid it in the first place. Ma's watch."

"A great day for a picnic," said his father. "Here, let's see the watch." He smiled and started to wind it.

"Oh, honey," said Steve's mother. "I'm so glad." She hugged Steve and kissed him.

"Fit as a fiddle—as a watch, I mean," said his father, holding the watch up to his ear. "Allow me, madam," he said, bowing to his wife as he put the watch around her wrist.

Steve glowed.

"As I mentioned before," said his father, "it's a great day for a picnic."

"You said it would turn up, Dad," said Steve. "I found the hidden treasure. I should really get to keep it," he added.

His parents looked at each other.

His mother nodded to his father.

"For your ninth birthday," said his father, "you'll have a watch of your own."

"Wrapped in a check?" laughed his mother.

"Oh, Ma!" said Steve.

"Let's get this picnic on the road," said his father.

"Don't you think you ought to finish shaving?" suggested his wife.

They all laughed.

In a little while the family was on its way, off for a great day in the country.

And what about Steve? Did he get into any more trouble?

Mmmm—well, you know how it is. Some days he did and some days he didn't. Good days and bad days, that's how it is.

ABOUT THE AUTHOR

May Garelick was three years old when she first came to New York. She has lived in many parts of the United States, but this city remains her favorite place.

"I love the city," she says, "and the country can be pretty exciting, too. I like big adventure, but I think the biggest adventure of all is the one of day-to-day living, and so I wrote this story of an average boy and his life with his family in a city apartment."

Miss Garelick is an editor in a New York publishing house. She is the author of *Manhattan Island* and *What's Inside: The Story of an Egg That Hatched,* and the coauthor of two cookbooks for children.

ABOUT THE ARTIST

Arthur Getz was born in New Jersey and now makes his home in New York. He financed his studies at the Pratt Institute with summer jobs as a seaman aboard a freighter that took him from New York to the West African coast. During World War II he served as a first lieutenant with the United States Army in the Philippines. Mr. Getz is a painter and magazine artist whose work appears regularly on the cover of *The New Yorker*.